Hollywood Lied

Iris Carden

Ipswich, Qld, Australia
ISBN 978-0-6484256-9-4
A catalogue record for this book is available at the
National Library of Australia.

Mary Elizabeth Marsdensen

It began with Mary Elizabeth Marsdensen. That was a name the whole world came to know, but only after she was dead.

She went to the Emergency Department at Brisbane General Hospital on a busy Friday night. When the triage nurse, Adrian Hughes, asked what she was there for, Ms Marsdensen simply said: "I'm dead. What's supposed to happen now? Do I go to the morgue or something?" She coughed and looked pleadingly at the nurse.

Nurse Hughes took the obvious action. He called for the people in the white coats. Pink scrubs to be more accurate. That was the uniform of the nursing staff in the Mental Health Emergency Clinic at the time.

In MHEC there was some excitement about Ms Marsdensen's arrival, after all Cotard's Syndrome is very rare. The psychiatric registrar tried to explain to the new patient that she only believed she was dead. In reality she was quite alive. She very carefully explained that Ms Marsden had a neurological condition, and that she most likely had lesions in her frontal lobe. It could be treated with antidepressants and other mood modulating drugs. If the drugs didn't work, there was always the option to use electro shock therapy, or to operate on the lesions when they were located. There was no need to worry. A few days in the psych unit to begin medication and get stable, a consultation or two with a neurologist to see whether or not to operate on the lesion, and Ms Marsdensen would be well on the way to recovery.

It was some hours before Ms Marsdensen persuaded a nurse to do what would have been done automatically if she'd been admitted for a physical, rather than mental, illness: to take her pulse and temperature. The nurse complied, thinking it would help prove to the patient that she really was alive.

It proved she was not.

Instantly, Mary Elizabeth Marsdensen became a prized scientific specimen, and the world's most famous woman. She had no pulse, no blood pressure, her temperature varied with the temperature of whatever room she was in.

An EEG, MRI, CT and numerous other members of the medical alphabet confirmed that she had some brain activity, but it was vastly different to normal human brain activity, and that there was, indeed, a lesion, the size of a grape, in her brain. She had no blood circulation, and no other normal bodily functions, except movement, and mysteriously speech even though she wasn't breathing. It would later be discovered that although she wasn't breathing, she still had enough muscle control to pull air into her lungs to use for speech. The air she breathed in didn't oxygenate blood, of course, because there was no blood circulating to be oxygenated.

Non-scientists, reading the news the next morning, noted the oddness of the story, but failed to understand the full import of what was explained, or what it would mean for the future.

Many scientists also missed the importance of the event. Others, like microbiologist Dr Martin Pryce, realised it was of ultimate importance. Dr Pryce contacted the hospital to ask for blood and other samples from Ms Marsdensen, and results of all tests. Then he called his long-time friend and recently-retired colleague Dr Robert Beare to come out of retirement for this major project.

The Pryce-Beare study would be the first of many into the mysterious condition Ms Marsdensen presented at the hospital with that night. It would be a long time before anyone knew just how significant this particular study would be.

At 7am, Nurse Hughes clocked off from his shift. He had a headache. Headache was an understatement. At home he told his wife it felt like fireworks going off in his frontal lobe. And he felt tired, more tired than he ever remembered being. He felt as if every single part of his body was tired. Even his bones felt tired, and he could feel every single tired bone. He had just started to develop an annoying cough.

"Must be the flu that's going around," his wife, Marianne, said practically. She kissed him good-bye and left for work at a nearby primary school. By lunchtime, she would start to get a killer headache, too...

Hollywood Lied

Hollywood had told us what to expect. So much so, that when it really happened, we didn't recognise it at first. Hollywood lied. The zombie apocalypse wasn't about people constantly running from place to place, trying to avoid being bitten or eaten by ravenous monsters. Society didn't collapse, it just metamorphosed.

It started with the flu pandemic. Bird flu and swine flu had been bad, but the panic about Ebola had been so out-of-proportion to the reality everywhere but west Africa, that everyone was well and truly tired of panics about the latest superbug. So the warnings about the expected new flu that everyone was urged to be immunised against, were pretty much ignored. Besides, it was only the flu, right?

Then Mary Elizabeth Marsdensen reported into the hospital dead, having contracted the flu at about the time she returned from an overseas holiday.

As it turned out, the vaccinations weren't any good against what this flu mutated into anyway. Nobody had been prepared for zombie flu. That's what we came to call it. Scientifically it was H3N5+, but we all called it Zombie Flu, or Zedflu. Droplets from a cough or a sneeze were enough to cause infection. Someone next to you in the street could cough, and kill you days later, and then we found out there were worse things than death.

People got sick with the flu, really sick. They started with the migraine to end all migraines. Really, it was the flu virus taking over and making its home in the brain. Antivirals didn't help. The next symptom was incredible fatigue, joint pain, and then a horrible rattling cough producing copious amounts of mucus. Most victims died from respiratory or other complications. Then, about 36 hours later, they got up and started moving around again.

People the virus had started to attack were infectious from when the cough started, up until death, and beyond. They were infectious when they were still just normal people with a cough, still your sister, your brother, your neighbour, your boss, the woman next to you at the checkout line.

It started with Mary Elizabeth Marsdensen, but it spread fast. Within days, there were cases reported all over the world. Scientists posited that she had probably spread the flu around the Brisbane International Airport when she returned from her holiday - thereby giving it to people who were going to almost every place on earth. There's nothing a pandemic loves more than international travel.

Pandemics also love hospitals, full of people with weakened immune systems, that are taken by surprise. By the time the Brisbane Hospital got control of things and stopped the spread of the virus within the hospital - almost half the staff and patients had succumbed to Zedflu. From the hospital, to staff members' families and friends and schools and hobbies, it took a very firm hold in our city, very quickly.

At first, the deadheads were treated as medical miracles, people who were alive, but shouldn't be. They were locked in padded rooms, and doctors discussed how to treat the mental illness that came with resurrection.

That's the other part of Mary Elizabeth Marsdensen's story. With no blood circulation or respiration, her body deteriorated. At the same time the lesion in her brain grew larger and larger. Her behaviour became more and more irrational as the mass inside her skull filled more and more of the enclosed space. When she presented at the hospital, the lesion in her brain was the size of a grape. A day later, when the mass in her brain was the size of a golf ball, she was lost the ability to speak. The day after that, when it was the size of an apple, she took a bread knife from the dining table and plunged it into the base of another patient's throat. From then on, she had to be kept in a secure room. For the next week and a half, until the decomposition was finally enough to prevent her doing anything, she took every opportunity to try to kill any human she came into contact with.

Once the supply of padded rooms ran out, the debate began about whether the deadheads were really alive or dead. The churches and other some other religious groups proclaimed life and demanded that they receive appropriate care.

Civil authorities found it more practical to prevent "resurrections". A new Public Health Management Law mandated that everyone, not just Zedflu victims, had to be cremated within 24 hours of death. It was the most humane way. Burying people who might experience a fortnight or so of "life" after death was just cruel (and risked that compassionate families or friends might try to dig up their loved ones.) That's what we do now. Of course, when people die alone and are not found, no-one knows to cremate them. Those ones are a problem.

So, this is the world we live in today, my world. Unlike Hollywood's vision of a zombie apocalypse, the Zedflu didn't cause society to break down. It just changed things a bit. Everyone who can work online from home does so. No-one goes out if they can avoid it. When people do go out, we all suit up – disposable suits, of course. It's easy to get a seat on public transport now, and we all have healthier diets now that everyone eats at home.

In all honesty, for me personally, nothing very much changed at all.

In my street, we have a code. Everyone hangs a towel out their window by 8am and takes it in again by 8pm. We watch each other's houses. If the towels go out and come in, we know the people in the houses are still human and rational. If they don't, we call the Health Management Team. Most neighbourhoods have systems like this.

No-one is going to die at home and just not be found now, we're all interested in the welfare of our neighbours in a way we never were before. We don't want deadheads in our street, spreading the lethal virus, breaking into houses, slaughtering people, or even just generally rampaging and destroying property.

We stay constantly linked through the internet. We still have all the social media we had before Zedflu, but a new one, Evision has come along. Evision was a super-upgrade to the Skype and VOIP phones. If we usually talk to someone regularly on Evision, and they don't answer, we call the Health Management Team then, too. It's not that anyone likes dobbing friends and loved ones in to be cremated, it's just that the alternative is much, much worse.

Off the Grid

The supermarket delivery is here. I watch through the window, as the delivery man piles the bags up beside my front door. I think it's a man. The white disposable suits everyone wears when we have to be among other people make it hard to tell. He waves to me through the window, and I wave back. I wait and watch my groceries. Zedflu can only survive outside the human body for 30 minutes. I watch to ensure no other humans approach my groceries for half an hour, before I suit up go out and collect them. In the front room I carefully remove my suit, gloves last, pulling them inside out as I remove them, so I don't touch the outside. Everything goes through the chute to hazardous waste bin.

I know I haven't been near another human being. I know I'm not contaminated, but I am still just as careful as if someone had coughed over me while I was outside the door. It's become habit, and it's a habit that can help me stay alive. As I said, my life hasn't changed much. I've always been a careful person. I just have this extra thing to be careful about now.

I've heard there's a couple of companies selling delivery boxes – with a numbered coded lock – delivery people drop the shopping in the box from outside the house, and the householder can collect through another door inside the house. The code is given out with the order. It saves going outside to collect groceries or other deliveries. I might get one, but it means having workers come into my house. I'm not sure if I want to take that risk.

I'm luckier than many people. My back yard has a very high, solid fence. Deadheads aren't known for being particularly athletic, at least not once they reach the point where they become violent, so there's no real worry one will climb the fence. It means I can go outside without a suit, just not out the front. I've got a couple of fruit trees out there – so I have some food that I know automatically isn't contaminated. I don't have to watch it for half an hour before I can collect and eat it. I have solar power as well, so the power outages don't bother me, the way they do a number of other households in our street. When I got the battery storage system for my solar power, and went completely off-grid, some friends thought I was going a bit far with the environmental thing. Those friends are dead now, dead and cremated. They all caught the flu at a party that I bailed out on at the last minute. I guess I had the last laugh there. I was never really big on parties, or other social gatherings.

I have rainwater tanks as well – another thing I did for the environment but am particularly glad of now. So far there's never been any interruption to the water service, but who knows what will happen, as the population keeps shrinking and there are fewer and fewer workers out there. All my life, the news kept up a running commentary of the unemployment rate. The unemployment problem's fixed now. Now the news reports the number of unfilled jobs.

I have a large house, as well as a large yard. I did well in buying it. I'd had visions of one day having children, maybe. Maybe I just liked having my own little world, where I could write in peace, locked away from everyone. I have everything I need, as long as there are still enough delivery people to bring me food. Maybe I should order more food plants for the yard, just in case the supply of delivery people runs out. There's plenty of space, I can turn it into a food-producing jungle, get even further off the grid. Relying on other people is risky in this world.

In some ways the Zedflu is good for me. Television is hard to watch with all the actors in disposable biohazard suits. No-one can tell one character from another. There are a couple of shows with actors in ordinary clothes – but they are expensive to produce with high biosecurity measures imposed on cast and crew. There's not a lot of those shows. Of course, there's re-runs from the golden age that we didn't know was so golden, before Zedflu, but how often can you see the same episode of Midsomer Murders? No-one goes out very much, so what's left to do but read? My book sales are going very well, thank you very much. Not the physical copies, very few of those go, but eBooks – they're flying off the virtual shelves.

I know some people, especially older people, have trouble managing to use the internet. I feel sorry for them. Hopefully, the old people have all moved in with their younger family members by now or moved into old people's homes. Do old people's homes still exist? I haven't heard anything about that. If Zedflu got into one of those, it would spread like wildfire. Maybe they're all dead. Dead and cremated, hopefully.

As for me, I've always lived a fair share of my life on-line. I've never actually met anyone at my publishing company in person. It's so easy to just write a manuscript and email it through. Come to think of it, I've had my groceries delivered since long before the Zedflu pandemic. My car is ten years old and has less than 50,000km on the clock. I've always just preferred to stay home, in my own space, and write.

I don't know what happens if the internet goes down. I guess there's no more work for me, and no more deliveries. That's another good reason to order more food plants while I can. Maybe I should build a stockpile of things like toilet paper, canned food, washing powder, and biohazard suits. There are some things I just can't produce at home, but the further off the grid I can get, the better. Only a year ago, that would have made me sound like some kind of "survivalist loon". I bet the loons are laughing their faces off now.

Health Inspector

There is a knock on the door. This is unexpected. The delivery person's already been. I'm not expecting anything else. Through the window, I can see someone in a biohazard suit standing outside my door, and not showing any signs of leaving.

"Hello?" I call out.

"Hello," said a deep, masculine voice. "My name's Ted, I'm the new health inspector for this area. Just stopping by for a health check."

He holds up an identity badge to the window. The badge says he is Dr Edward Beare from Queensland Health. The photo is of a man with deep brown eyes, almost black, dark hair and the kind of tan that is inherited rather than from sun exposure. I guess Indian heritage. It's a very handsome face. I look from the photo to the biohazard suit now standing outside my window. The eyes are the same, so dark, like endless depths, black holes that no light can escape.

"Ted Beare?" I ask, incredulous.

"Yeah, my father had a sense of humour, and my mother didn't know much English."

"Most unfortunate." I say. "So, what is this health check? I don't have Zedflu."

"It's not just about the flu," he says. Yeah, I'll bet. "The Health Department's concerned that people aren't going out to their local doctors as much as they should, so the Department's sending out doctors to do regular primary health checks."

"I'm fine," I say. "And I'm not letting you or any other doctor in."

"That's OK. I just have a quick questionnaire here. You are Angela Amelia Tynehurst?"

"Yes, that's me."

He looks at his clipboard for a moment, as something seems to dawn on him. "A.A. Tynehurst? The author? You wrote the Farnsedale books?"

"Yes, but is that really on your questionnaire?"

"Oh, no. Sorry. It's just.... I love your work. I know this is unusual, but could I have your autograph?"

"What?"

"If I bring a copy of one of your books and leave it here. You could come out and autograph it, and I could pick it up later. Is that OK? I have the weekend off. I could leave the book on Saturday morning and come back later in the afternoon."

"You'd actually go outside, on your day off, twice, just to get my autograph?"

"Well, yes. If that's OK." He seems to be blushing, but with his skin tone, and the little bit of his face I can see, it's hard to tell.

"Sure," I say.

"Oh, great, thanks so much, I'll see you on Saturday." He trips on his own feet as he starts to back away from the window.

"One minute," I call out.

"Yes?"

"Don't you have questions to ask me?"

He looks confused for a moment, then looks at his clipboard. "Oh yes."

We go through a standard set of questions and answers about medical history, surgeries, medications, any diagnoses of chronic illness, lifestyle, diet, exercise, who my regular GP is. Actually, it seems this might be about more than Zedflu, but maybe that's just to make people feel safer about revealing any symptoms they might have. Queensland Health does send out the Health Management Teams to deal with deadheads, after all.

"I'm leaving a card with a log-on for your personal health site here, a blood pressure test machine, and a thermometer here. Could you please log on in the next 24 hours and list your height, weight, blood pressure and temperature? It just gives us a baseline, in case you need medical care at any time. Oh, and I need to take your temperature now. Just stand still and I'll use thermo-imaging to check."

I stand still while he aims something that looks like a camera at the window.

"All good," he says. "I'll see you Saturday."

"Sure," I answer. "It's a date."

He waves as he walks away.

Fans. Who would have thought any of them would be dedicated enough to go out of the house when they didn't have to, just to get me to sign a book? I never understood why they'd all rush to bookshops to have me sign their books in the old days. They had the book, that was my creative work, a signature wasn't exactly creative or challenging or difficult, or particularly worth having. Book signings are a part of the job I don't really miss. But Dr Ted Beare really wants his book signed...and really, it's not going to cost me any more than a disposable biohazard suit.

Interesting-looking man that Dr Ted Beare. Those eyes are fascinating. Perhaps I can add him to a new novel.

I'm sure I could build an interesting character on the little I know of him. He's intelligent enough to be a doctor, but instead of being a regular GP and just seeing most of his patients over Skype or Evision, he's risking his life, checking on people who might not have been in contact with their GPs. He's risking his life for people like me. Maybe he can be a new love interest for Farnsedale, now that I've killed off Detective Cogburn? Not that Cogburn's much of a loss – Farnsedale can do much better. She needs someone much more her equal. Intelligent, courageous and handsome. Maybe Dr Beare could be a base for a character with possibilities. Of course, I'd have to give him a far more believable name. Fiction always has to be so much more believable than reality. (Dr Beare? Why does that sound familiar?)

Thinking about Farnsedale and her abysmal love life reminds me of that interview with News Breakfast. Tiffany asked me: "So, there's one question everyone wants answered. Is Farnsedale's terrible track record with love a reflection of Tynehurst's?"

Of course, I'd answered, "Not at all. Farnsedale keeps looking for love. Tynehurst doesn't have the time, she's too busy writing the next novel." The audience had laughed.

I wonder what kind of man I would have loved, if I'd had the opportunity? It's not going to happen now, of course. The world has changed. People don't meet people any more. We are all just locked away safely in our own little cocoons. It's no great loss, not really. My first love was always writing. Words have always welcomed me and soothed me, whatever is happening. I think I already said, I'm better off than most people. Modern life must be hell for extroverts. As long as I can write, I'm pretty much content.

Saturday

I hear a tapping at my front window. A figure in a
biohazard suit holds up my book. Dr Ted Beare calls out
a greeting and says he'll leave the book and be back in a
couple of hours.

"That's fine," I call out. "I'll see you then."

Half an hour later, when I open the door, I find not just
the book, the latest Farnsedale, but a massive bouquet of
red roses I hadn't seen through the window.

I sign the book and bring the roses inside. It's a very
long time since anyone's given me flowers, and these are
exquisite.

The card with the flowers simply says: "Is it OK if I
Evision you this evening?"

I guess I have until he comes to pick up the book, to
come up with my answer. Is he just a friendly man, an
obsessed fan, a potentially dangerous stalker? Does he
want to talk about my books? Or what? What kind of
man goes out unnecessarily at great personal risk, just to
contact me? Maybe I am overthinking this. It's just an
Evision call after all. If he says or does anything
disturbing, it doesn't take much to block him. (I've
blocked obsessive fans before.)

Is he a potential love interest for Tynehurst, rather than
Farnsedale? That's ridiculous. Farnsedale's fictional

world might still have people meeting, interacting, falling in and out of love. Tynehurst's world is one where human interaction is a life-threatening event.

I trim the rose stems and place them in a vase. It is very nice to be given roses. They are my favourite flowers. Maybe I could order rose plants to grow in the back yard? I could enjoy them all the time.

An Evision call with Dr Ted Beare? It's a long time since I've had even a virtual face-to-face conversation, at least one that wasn't about work. Don't get me wrong. I do have friends. We're just more the kind of friends who communicate through social media and email, rather than actually talking to each other. Would I have anything to talk about with a stranger? People used to do that. Just have casual conversations face to face. They still do it in books. I can write a casual conversation for Farnesdale easily enough. But that's fiction. It's something that people did in the old days. It's the world that people escape to in my books – where a serial killer is the worst danger anyone could think of. In the era of Zed-flu, how could anyone make small talk?

What would Farnesdale say if Dr Ted Beare had wanted to have a conversation with her? She'd agree, of course, and would make witty conversation. But Farnsedale carries a gun and isn't afraid of anything. She's confident, beautiful, intelligent, and tough as nails. I'm intelligent but fail on the rest of those things. A counsellor once suggested that Farnsedale was invented to cover my inadequacies. I gave up going to counselling. That really showed her.

If I'm honest about it, I wouldn't have known what to say if someone had asked me out for a coffee in the days before Zed-flu either. Part of the reason I'm such a prolific writer, is that I don't have romantic relationships, and I have friendships I can manage without too much personal contact. That leaves lots of time for writing.

Do I want to form any kind of friendship or relationship that requires actually talking to people? Now? In a world where human contact can be fatal? Of course, it's not actual human contact he's asking for, just an Evision call. And it would be nice to see what he actually looks like, after all the image on the ID badge was a very handsome man.

I'm overthinking this. It's just a yes or no question. Can he call me? How many thousand times in the history of the world has a man asked a woman if he could call her? How many women go into an hour-long internal debate over the answer to the question? I don't actually know the answer to any of those questions.

I can't agonise over the question any longer. He's already tapping at the window. It's time for an answer.

"Hello." I call. "Thank you for the roses, they're absolutely beautiful."

"You're welcome," he said. "I saw them at a roadside stand and hoped you would like them."

"You stopped at a roadside stand? Actually, bought flowers from another person?"

"Yes, the vendor was in a suit. I was in a suit. And the roses looked so nice."

"Well they do, but that was kind of a risk to take to get them."

"You haven't been out for a while, have you?" Dr Ted Beare asks me.

"Well, nobody goes out any more, if they have any other choice."

"I don't see the point of being locked inside and afraid all the time. Besides, it's safer now that cremations are happening so quickly. There's not much fear of deadheads attacking, and suits and masks make it safe to interact with live people. It's why the Health Department decided it was safe to start sending doctors into the community."

People are going out, when they don't absolutely have to. I'm trying to process the idea.

"Er, what do you do when you're out?" I ask sceptically.

"Anything you can do in a suit and mask. So not swimming or dining at a restaurant, but walking, going to movies, visiting parks and museums; just getting out of the house."

"I'm not sure if I'd be willing to take that kind of risk."

"How about an Evision conversation, then? There's no risk of infection, and it's easier than talking through a closed window."

Have we yelled all of this at each other through a closed window? How silly is that? When we could so easily talk face to face, at least virtually, over Evision.

"Yes, of course." I find myself saying. Was this the decision that was so difficult? Of course, I want to talk to Ted, and I want to hear more about what has been going on outside – even if I'm not about to go out and see for myself.

Evision

I'm waiting by the computer for my Evision call from
Ted. Ted. When did he become "Ted"?

I am reminded of a teenaged me waiting beside a
landline telephone for a call from a boy. Is this the same
thing? Surely not. I'm a mature woman. I'm just looking
forward to a conversation with another intelligent adult,
one who has been out into the world I avoid.

Looking behind me, I wonder if the writing studio is
really the best place for this conversation. I love the
studio, but it's not quite the place you'd have a
conversation with a guest. The entire wall behind me is
painted with chalkboard paint, and covered in my notes,
thought bubbles, ideas, whatever comes into my head
and doesn't fit exactly what I'm writing at the moment.

I wonder what he will think of it? Should I move to a
more inviting room?

Too late - the green light is flashing at the corner of my
screen.

I click "accept" and take a deep breath.

Ted Beare's face appears on the screen. To be honest, I
don't even notice where he is, what's behind him on the
screen. I'm caught up, looking at that handsome gently-
shaped face, those deep brown eyes.

I've never been good at casual conversation, but somehow, we manage to talk about everything and nothing. His mother was a jeweller in Mumbai, not the kind of jeweller that just sold jewellery and repaired watches. She designed and crafted jewels to be works of art in and of themselves. His father, a molecular biologist, had been there for a conference when his watch stopped working. He walked into a little jeweller's next to the hotel he was staying at, and the rest was history.

Ted had grown up in South Brisbane and gone to UQ. He was always going to end up doing something in the biomedical field. Either that or be an artist like his mother. His mother knew enough English to get by, but never really mastered the idiosyncrasies of Australian English - so Ted and his father had endless fun with idioms such as "don't come the raw prawn" and "going off like a frog in a sock".

Me? I'd grown up in Rockhampton, Central Queensland. My life hadn't been quite the same as his. No one in my family had ever gone to university before me. Yes, I'd always known I wanted to write. I'd fallen in love with books from early childhood.

My fist book was finished when I was in grade 10 and was never published. At 15, I learned just how disappointing a rejection slip could be, and I had a very good collection of very disappointing slips that said things like "our lists are already full". I had imagined knights on horseback in the lists, ready to joust for the honour of having a book published, or an endless list of good and bad authors similar to Santa's list of good and bad children. (If I was on the "bad" list would I always be on the bad list?)

It was years before I learned just how hard it could be to get a writing deal. And that it paid to be persistent. You could try ten publishers and the eleventh would buy the book. Well maybe not that first book It really was awful.

We laugh. We talk about our pasts. We talk about how Zedflu had changed our lives and discovered that neither of us has really changed a lot. I had always lived and worked in a fairly solitary style, working from home, not going out much. Even in primary school, the cool solitude of an air-conditioned library had been more inviting than the playground.

He has always loved being out among people and doesn't see fear of a disease to be any reason to change that. What I had initially taken for courage, was simply him being the person he was. He tells me he has been to India numerous times to visit his mother's family. In India, there was never much of a chance to be alone. His mother had been one of seven children. Her mother had been one of ten. There were cousins and other relatives who were just called cousins everywhere. He loved those times and found being an only child when he was at home in Brisbane to be nowhere near as fun. He understands that his mother's generation learned about population control, but still likes to imagine what life would have been like if he lived with half a dozen playmates. The one thing that really has changed for him since the pandemic began, is that his parents have died. His father came out of retirement to help work on a cure for the Zedflu, an accident in the lab exposed him to the disease. Ted's mother refused to stay away from her husband, and so caught the disease from him. They had both insisted their only child stay away from them once they were infected. His last conversations with them were over Evision. He went with the Health Management Team to collect their bodies for cremation.

We are complete opposites. I love living in my cocoon, he is the butterfly always out doing things being among others of his own type. He can't imagine not having regular contact with other people. I can't imagine having it. But.... But there's something. There's something in how he is so enthusiastic, how happy he is with his life, despite the threat all around him, despite working in an occupation that could easily bring him into contact with deadheads. Despite it all, he thrives. Maybe I'd like a little of what it is that seems to give him so much life and energy and enthusiasm. Maybe just a little. Not too much. I don't want to go far out of my cocoon.

So, when he asks if I'd like to go for a walk sometime, I find myself agreeing, at the same time as asking myself if I have gone totally insane? Where will we go?

The botanical gardens are beautiful, and hardly anyone will be there. Lots of people prefer to stay home or commute between home and work without stopping anywhere to enjoy the world around them. I understand their attitude but suddenly I have a craving to go and visit the gardens, I haven't been there since, well, since a long time before the Zedflu broke out.

We make a time. Tomorrow, a Sunday afternoon walk in the public gardens. What could be better? A Sunday afternoon walk, while wearing a disposable biohazard suit.

Just A Walk in the Park

Do I wear make-up? Will my mask just mess it up anyway?

The TV's on while I'm pondering. Breaking news, a massive house fire. A massive house, on a massive fire. The television image shows three fire engines, a number of firefighters in heavy duty protective gear. A reporter in a regular disposable biohazard suit is talking to a police officer in the blue uniform protective suit.

There were five people in the house. Two adults and three children including a newborn. The blaze was so high so fast that there was no hope of saving anyone, and arson was definitely suspected. Relatives had reported that the baby had a cough yesterday, and the mother had been frantic. No-one said it, but it was heavily implied that either the parents had set the fire so Zedflu wouldn't get the whole family, or neighbours had heard about the sick child and set the fire.

Five people died because a baby had a cough, that may or may not have been Zed-flu. I'm cold. This is the reality of the world outside my home. Dare I go out today? Just for a walk in the botanical gardens? What if something happens? What if I am confronted with someone who has Zed-flu and my suit is compromised in some way? What if there's a deadhead loose and attacking people? I know that's not supposed to happen as often now, but not as often doesn't mean never.

Is this really worth it?

I think of my conversation with Ted yesterday. I have to admit that I haven't felt so happy in a very long time. And I really do want to see him again. Is happiness worth the risk of going outside? Is anything? I know lots of people go outside for their work. Or they have to go for family or other important commitments. But I don't have a compelling reason, just wanting to spend time with someone really isn't that urgent. Maybe we could just talk over Evision again.

Courage is not something that comes easily to me. But what is courage but the determination to go ahead and do something even knowing there is a risk? Today, I find I am more courageous than I thought I could be. I may not have a compelling, desperately important reason for going out, but I do have a reason, and yes, it is reason enough.

I say a silent prayer for the family who died in the house fire. A whole family fallen to Zed-flu even if no family member actually had it. I wonder about the arsonist. Was it some neighbour or relative? Worse, was it one of the parents, realising that if the baby was coughing in the house, it was likely that everyone had been exposed? How much fear does it take to kill a house full of people?

For practical reasons, it's a no on the make-up. It's also a no on the rest of the news. I turn off the television. Some truths are just not worth knowing.

Ted is going to meet me here. We'll drive to the Gardens to go for our walk. It would be nice to pack a picnic. I can't remember the last time I had a picnic anywhere. Of course, I'm not actually going to do that. After all, to eat would mean removing my mask.

So I guess it doesn't matter what I wear, and it doesn't matter about make-up, because what Ted's going to see is a white disposable biohazard suit. Great. Well, the Zed-flu certainly didn't do much for the fashion industry, did it?

Do I need a hat, I wonder? Does this suit protect from UV as well?

No time to worry, since there's a knock at the door now anyway. I wave at Ted through the window and call out that I'm just putting my suit on.

As we leave, I notice that the house across the road does not have a towel hanging out the front window. I mention it to Ted.

"Maybe they slept in." He says, "Don't worry about it unless the towel still isn't out when we get back."

The Gardens really are beautiful. I don't think plants have ever looked more beautiful. I really do have a lot to learn about gardening if I ever want to make my little backyard haven anything like this amazing place. I don't think I ever really appreciated that it was here before.

Ted and I walk, and we talk, about everything and nothing, about the news this morning, about the way people are changing - not just people who have Zed-flu, but people who are becoming increasingly paranoid. I have to admit, I'm probably one of them. But would I have set light to a family's home, just in case? Maybe I'm not as paranoid as some.

We see very few people in the Gardens. There is a person walking a dog. I can't tell from the distance we are whether the person is a woman or a man. I think about that, the need for people to get out and do basic things like exercising their pets. I suppose people still get out and run as well - at least some would. We pass a couple of gardeners - in their heavy-duty suits, planting out seedlings. Somehow it seems sad that, so few people will appreciate their work. I decide I will come back to see the plants when they're grown.

Down at the duck pond, little turtle beaks keep breaking the water as we watch. There was a time when people on the bank of the pond meant food being thrown to the turtles. It looks as if they haven't forgotten. Why didn't I think to bring some bread or something for them?

While I'm thinking of things I had forgotten, something comes to me. The flu comes and goes. It always has. Bird flu went away when flu season was over. Why has Zed-flu stayed around? Ted's a doctor, does he know?

He' tells me, there's a lot of people researching it, beginning with the Pryce-Beare study that started as soon as Mary Elizabeth Marsdensen went into hospital. (I suddenly remember where I heard of "Dr Beare" before.) Scientists don't really have a lot of answers, just a few theories, and a lot of questions. Zed-flu came, and it didn't go away. No-one who had it got better, so no-one's got any resistance. Work on a vaccination isn't getting anywhere. For now the only thing was have to combat it is isolation. Keeping people from spreading the infection is the best way to stop it going any further. That's why everyone's wearing suits. Eventually, there won't be any more cases. But there will be a while before that happens.

We still have a population of homeless people who can't hide away in their homes and stay isolated from infection. We still have people who say they never catch the flu, so they won't wear a suit when they're out (although we are getting fewer of those over time), we still have people who take risks. Aren't we taking a risk now? Not really, we're wearing suits. We're safe from droplets. That's the real danger, now that the dead are cremated before they can become a problem.

No droplets, no spread of Zed-flu, we're doing our part to overcome the disease. And we're safe. So, we may as well enjoy the Gardens, and the sunshine.

Safe - it's a word I don't hear a lot of nowadays. Certainly, it's a word the news doesn't use very much.

Suddenly I feel safe. Really safe. I relax and enjoy the day.

It's dark by the time Ted drops me at home. I go inside and remove my suit and drop it in the chute. Then I take in my towel from the window, so the neighbours don't call the Health Management Team.

I'm safe, but now I'm wondering about the people who don't have a safe, secure home to go to. What are they doing tonight?

The Curious Incident of the Neighbour in the Night Time

It's a couple of days since the outing to the Gardens. Ted and I have talked every night either on the phone or by Evision. I find I'm looking forward to our conversations throughout the day.

The house across the road has had the towel in and out at the appropriate times ever since that day, so I guess that's all right. It's late, I've just showered and I'm ready for bed.

There's a noise out at the front of the house. I look through the window. I see a woman without a suit on. I recognise her. She lives across the road. I don't know her name, but I've seen her around.

She has a rock and she's hitting the large window beside the door. I suddenly realise I should have put a security screen there. I have security screens on all the windows that can be opened. (When I put my towel out each day, I have to poke it between the bars of the screen. I had never thought of this strip of glass beside the door. It doesn't open, it just lets me see who is on the other side of the door. I run to the bedroom, shutting as many doors as possible between myself and the entry way.

I hear the crash, and know the window is broken.

I grab my mobile phone from beside the bed and call triple 0. It seems an eternity before the operator come s on the line and asks if I want Police, Ambulance of Fire Brigade. I can hear things being thrown around in my lounge room and I say, "Police, Urgent."

In a moment I'm speaking to the police operator. Why operator after operator? Isn't this supposed to be an emergency number? I'm told to push some heavy furniture against the door and don't leave the room until the police tell me it's OK. The operator will stay on the line while I barricade the door.

I put all my weight against a chest of drawers and it takes everything I have to move it but it's against the door. I get back to the phone, and the operator says he'll stay on the line with me until it's safe.

I'm sitting on the floor leaning on the chest of drawers, I have never been this frightened in my life. I'm shaking and crying and desperately want this to all be over.

Eventually I hear sirens. Blue lights shine through the bedroom window, reflect on the mirror, and give the whole room an eerie pulsating blue colour. Everything's blue. I hear the ruckus, voices shouting. More scuffling, more things being broken, I think. What's happening out there? I really want to know, but of course, I'm not going to take a look. Eventually I hear the words "All clear".

A voice on the other side of the bedroom calls: "Miss Tynehurst? It's safe now. Stay in there for at least half an hour before you come out. We'll keep an officer here until the emergency repairs are done. A glazier's been called for the window." The operator leaves me now. I know there's a police officer outside the door, but without the voice on the phone as well, I feel very alone, and very vulnerable.

"Someone's coming now? In the middle of the night, to replace my window?" I hardly recognise my own shaking voice. It's almost midnight and I'm incredulous.

"Yes, this happens quite a bit," the voice on the other side of the door calls. "I recommend you get a proper security screen installed first thing in the morning."

"Absolutely. It's my top priority."

"I'm afraid you've got a few things broken, but at least you're safe. You weren't exposed at all?"

"No, I ran in here as soon as I saw her at the window."

"That's a smart move. Too many people decide to fight and defend their property. It never ends well. I'll leave you my card with the report number for this incident. You'll need it for your insurance claim, for the damage done. The glassier will leave a bill as well - they're used to waiting for the insurance to pay them out."

"Just how often does this happen?"

"Two or three times a week. I think there's a news truck coming up the street. Sorry, they ignore these most of the time, but you being famous and all."

I close the curtains on my bedroom window. I don't need cameras filming me in my pyjamas. My house may be the top news story in the morning, but my pink poodle pjs don't have to be part of the vision with the story.

I sit on my bed, knees pulled up under my chin and my arms around my legs, waiting. Eventually the police officer knocks on the door and calls out that the house is secure. It's been more than half an hour since they took the deadhead out, so it's safe to leave the room. He wishes me a good night.

Listening at the bedroom window, I hear reporters throwing questions at the police officer as he leaves.

Once again, I put all my weight against the chest of drawers, my back is against it and I'm pushing against the floor with my feet. It's much harder to move it this time, I guess the adrenaline isn't flowing so well now.

I try to avoid walking past any windows with open curtains as I inspect the damage. It's really not as bad as I expected. The bookshelf's smashed and the books have been thrown around, and a quite expensive vase is now a pile of porcelain chunks, with water over the carpet and roses thrown around the room. The roses had been starting to wilt anyway, I guess it was time to throw them out. Glass from photo frames has been shattered, and a coffee table is broken. Remarkably, the television's intact. I turn on the news channel, see the front of my house, and turn it off again.

Not all that long ago, I'd felt safe outside, walking in a public place. Now my little secure fortress doesn't even feel safe.

I wonder what will happen to my neighbour. Maybe I should have asked the police officer. Will she be cremated while she's still "alive" and fighting? Will she be locked up until she decomposes enough to not move anymore? Is there a humane way to treat an animated dead body?

I definitely will get the security screen installed first thing in the morning. Maybe I could get my fence extended so that instead of a safe yard at the back of the house, I just have a fortress all around. I could have a security camera installed so I can see who is outside. I would have a larger safe area. But would I feel safe even with that? Will I ever feel safe again?

There's still lights and noise out in front - obviously the media are still here. I do what I've always done in a crisis. I find a pen and paper and begin a list:

1. Security screen.
2. Front fence - secure.
3. Security cameras.

I stop a moment. Does "security cameras" mean that someone will come inside here, into my <u>house</u>? How else would they install it? I guess it couldn't be any more dangerous than last night. I realise I could have a delivery lock box installed in a front fence. I add a new item to my list:

4. Lock box.

Is that all? Is that what it takes to be safe? It doesn't feel safe.

Back in the bedroom, I move the chest of drawers for the third time tonight, barricading the door before I go to bed. Safe. What will it take to make me safe? Will I ever feel safe again?

Farnesdale would take this in her stride. She would have shot the neighbour, right through the frontal lobe, destroying the Zed-flu tumour, from an angle that ensured she wouldn't be exposed to blow-back of bodily fluids or brain matter. She'd have casually called in a clean-up team, had a glass of wine and gone easily to sleep.

It's kind of miserable, knowing I'll never measure up to my own fictional creation.

Aftermath

My house seems to be everywhere today, on every television station, all over the internet news sites.

If this happens two or three times per week, clearly it doesn't often happen to people who are moderately famous. I haven't seen coverage like this of anything in ages. I listen in to some of the reports, hoping to find out what actually happened to my deadhead neighbour. I guess it doesn't matter, I'm just curious.

At least one of the channels is broadcasting live from in front of my house, I know because behind the reporter I see the back of the man who is installing my security screen. Off camera, there's also a man measuring to extend my fence, so it encloses my whole yard - not just behind the house. He can do me a deal - he'll add in the delivery box and the security camera and two way communications system, at a discount. (He's of course hoping that one of the reporters will notice him and want to speak to him on air - free advertising would compensate for any discount he gave me.)

Ted's called, a couple of times, just checking that I'm OK. I assure him I am. Just shaken. I'm looking around my house wondering what I can do now to start making it feel like as safe place again. My Booker award certificate needs a new frame. Would that make me feel better? It would make my home look a little more like my home. While I'm at it, I need frames for a couple of photos of my sister's family and one of an award ceremony where I felt I looked particularly nice. (Usually I feel I don't have much style at all. Yet another area Farnsedale beats me in.)

I could take them all out and to a professional picture framer. Or I could measure them, and order frames on-line, to frame them myself. It's a no-brainer. I' m not going out to a shop. Not any chance of that. I find a tape measure and get started.

I notice something odd. The worker doing the fence has stopped. He's in his car, with his mask off, eating. I can tell by the packaging what. So fast food restaurants are still going then, even if the fancy, sit-down ones are failing. Must be drive-through. I haven't realised that drive-throughs were still a thing but if the workers are all in suits, I guess it must be OK. I wonder why they don't advertise?

It's a little bit of the old world. The world of only a year or so ago, when people were free to go out and buy some greasy salty morsels that would both harden and clog their arteries, a world I thought was long gone. Maybe it's not gone so much as just a little more hidden?

I wonder what else is happening outside my home that I hadn't thought about? It doesn't matter, though. Farnesdale might be the type of person would go out and make the most of whatever was still available in the world around. Even Dr Ted Beare might be the kind of person who would go out and make the most of life outside in the big wide world. I'm not that type of person. If I had for a moment thought I might become that person, my mind was changed definitively last night. Now, I'm the person who strengthens the fortress and stays away from the world.

I start to think again about the whole self-sufficiency thing. I'm definitely ordering more food plants. More fruit trees. What do I need to start a vegetable garden? Should I get a watering system that will make it easier for me to keep everything properly watered?

Yes, it's time to bunker down. No more dangerous things like a walk in the Botanical Gardens for me. No checking out which junk food places might still be offering unhealthy delights via a hole in the wall. All that is for someone else. Me? I'm on lock - down, until the Zedflu finally passes, or there's a cure or a vaccine or whatever it will take to get rid of it for ever.

Am I OK? Ted keeps calling to ask. <u>Yes, I'm fine.</u> Or I will be, when I have my bigger, better fence and my secure windows. I'll be fine, just as long as I can keep the world out.

There's a reporter knocking on my window. I shake my head. No, I don't want to talk. If I speak to this one, the others will come over - it's like seagulls coming after your chips at the beach. When did I last eat chips at the beach? Well, the metaphor still holds. Throw a chip to one squawking seagull, and a hundred others will turn up, all squawking for your lunch.

I wonder what the gulls at the beach are doing for a living now? Scavenging from picnickers seems a bit unlikely. I guess the fishing trawlers must still go out, and there must still be scraps. Maybe the gulls have gone to compete with the pelicans at the docks. In my mind, I can see the boats, the gulls and pelicans, the beach. I can smell the salt, and the rotting seaweed that's been washed ashore. Honest truth? The beach isn't all that great. I'm fine here, in my house, where soon, I'll have a fence that prevents reporters knocking on my window.

The news has gone from a picture of my house (at last) to a picture of something under a microscope. It's Zedflu. A scientist is explaining the link between climate change and H3N5+. This strain of flu's been around for a while, without becoming severe enough to kill, or to create brain tumours, or to cause corpses to go on murderous rampages. It was already all around the world, but never a severe strain of influenza, until it had the perfect conditions.

All this is news to me. Having heard the story, I really thought Mary Elizabeth Marsdensen had been the first person to ever have H3N5, it turns out, she was just the first known case of our new super-version of it. It was really a H3N5+.

What changed, was the climate. We did enough damage to change the seasons, and our seasonal flu didn't leave at the end of its expected time. Instead it stuck around, mutated, spread from country to country and continued to mutate. This flu season's never going to be over. The scientist says it quite cheerily.

All along scientists have been sure climate change would not end life on earth, he happily explains, it would just cause it to evolve and mutate. Lots of scientists believed humans wouldn't be able to adapt fast enough, however, so Zedflu had been pretty much inevitable. Once humans have gone, nature can work on getting the planet to a new kind of balance that we can't mess up.

I'm resisting the urge to punch the screen. After all, the television survived a deadhead's assault on the house, it deserves to keep going a little longer. Are they giving up on finding a cure? Who are "they" anyway? The scientists who've been happily expecting humans to become extinct?

Would we have done something about climate change sooner, if we had known this was going to be the result? Who is "we" here? Is it me? The neighbour who recently visited me after her death? The politicians? Who is the "we" who should have done something before it came to this? And is this where it will end? What else is going to mutate into something that can kill off the human race?

The scientist on screen has a coughing fit. Everyone who has seen the public health advisories, which probably means everyone still alive, knows what the cough means. The reporters run from the desk they are talking to him over. When he stops coughing, he says, sounding quite proud: "It's an amazing thing, documenting the process of extinction for a dominant species."

It's too much for me. After last night. After seeing my house on that very same screen for half the morning. As the camera swings round to show two news presenters scrambling to check their biohazard suits for any break and being doused in disinfectant. I find myself curling up on the floor and crying. Ted is calling again. <u>No, I am definitely not OK.</u>

Zombie Apocalypse

"Can I come in?" Ted says from the front door.

I dither for a while. Then decision falls on the side of trusting this one person. After all, after my neighbour's visit last night, what could possibly go wrong?

Despite trusting Ted, I still put on a suit to let him in. So I guess it's a very conditional trust.

What does "not OK" entail, he wants to know.

It all comes pouring out, just how frightened I was last night, reporters being like seagulls, then the scientist on the news this morning.

"It's a bloody zombie apocalypse," I say. "How cliché is that? The whole world is living a bad horror movie script."

"It's not the apocalypse, just a plague. Human beings have faced and overcome them heaps of times in the past, and we'll get through this one too." Ted says.

"I wish I could make myself believe that."

"The scientist you heard was Martin Pryce. He was a friend of my father's. They worked together for years. Uncle Martin's been looking forward to the end of the world for as long as I can remember. He must be having a great time now that he actually has something to study with the potential to kill humans. Don't worry, he's not the only scientist working on this, and not all of them think it's hopeless."

"Pryce. The Pryce-Beare study. He was the person your dad was working with when he died?"

"Yeah. Dad was exposed to the virus. He shouldn't have been. He always did everything by the book, but somehow an accident happened. If anyone was going to have an accident, I would always have expected it to be Martin. Dad was always complaining that Martin was great at research but horrible at taking safety precautions."

"I think he has it now, anyway. Did you see the news? Hear his cough?"

"I missed it, but I've heard about it. I wouldn't put it past him to have deliberately infected himself to study the disease from the inside out."

"Is that what happened to your father?"

"Dad wouldn't have infected himself. It's possible something Martin did caused him to be infected, but I don't really know. I have my suspicions, but I can't prove them."

"I'm sorry."

"Now, what are we going to do with you? I see the fortifications are going up. I hope you're leaving a drawbridge in this castle."

"Drawbridge?"

"You're not just going to stay shut in here are you? We don't know how long the pandemic will keep going. You can miss out on a lot if you stay locked away."

"Staying locked away is exactly what I was planning to do. I'm not going out there again until it's all clear."

"All clear. No more cases? That could be a long time. We're starting to get it under control, but it's not fully going away for a while. It's everywhere on earth, so it's a big thing to manage. But we can try to prevent new cases, we can keep it contained. We've just got to wait it out."

"Wait it out."

"If everyone keeps their suits on when they're out, we cremate the dead as quickly as possible, basically stop feeding the beast, it will stop. The flu is still the flu. It goes from person to person. Stop it doing that, and it will end."

"But we're not stopping it yet, are we? The woman across the road. I never saw her go out without a suit. I don't think she went out at all. But she still caught it.

Everyone's being careful, but how careful is careful enough?"

"We are getting there. There's fewer and fewer cases all the time. Forget Martin Pryce and his doomsday theories. Sure, the flu season isn't ending, but this flu will."

"OK, but if all we can do is wait it out, I'm going to wait it out in my fortress."

"Well, if the fortress gets lonely, you can always call me," he said, placing his hand over mine.

That was when his phone buzzed. He looked at it, scowled, and answered it. "Hello Uncle Martin, I heard about your television performance today."

I couldn't hear what the voice on the other side said, only Ted's side of the conversation: "No, I've never really thought about research, that was Dad's field, not mine. ... The work I'm doing is important, too. ... It's not the risk it's... Martin, I'm with someone right now. I'll think about it, that's all I can promise."

He hung up.

"That was Martin Pryce?" I asked, fairly needlessly.

"That was Martin Pryce."

"And he wants?"

"Me, to help in his research, to take over Dad's old job."

"Surely you're not going to do that! You just said..."

"I know what I just said. And I do have my suspicions. And really, if I took the job, it would be to find out for sure what really did happen. That's what your detective Farnsedale would do, isn't it?"

"Farnsedale's a fictional character, she doesn't have a lot to lose. What about you?"

"My parents are dead. I don't really have any other family, any wife or girlfriend, anyone who particularly needs me." He paused, looking at me a moment. "Unless that changes, I really probably am the perfect person for the job. I told him I'd think about it. For now, that's all I'm going to do."

"Wouldn't you be better working with someone who was actually trying to solve the problem, instead of enjoying watching it play out?"

"Maybe, but that wouldn't tell me how the most meticulous and careful person I ever knew came to be exposed to a virus he was studying."

I can see his point, and yes, it really is the type of thing Farnesdale would do, but Farnesdale is a product of my imagination. I don't want to see Ted risk his life for information that won't change the past, and working with this particular researcher, probably won't help the future either.

Inevitable

I guess it was inevitable. Ted took the job. I tried to talk him out of it. He has a very stubborn streak, and is really not willing to give up now that the idea has set in. He says any research will help with an eventual cure or preventative, and it really matters to him to find out how his father was exposed to the virus in that lab.

Ted tries to reassure me about his new colleague: it's been a week, and Dr Pryce is still coughing, but not showing any other symptoms, so whatever is causing his cough, it's not Zedflu. I'm not particularly reassured.

My fence is up and my home is now a fortress. Some part of me wants to persuade Ted to come and stay safe inside the fortress with me, but that's never going to happen.

Instead, I invite him to dinner. Am I insane? He's working in that lab, now, the one where his father contracted Zedflu, and I'm not only inviting him into my home, but into my home to eat. Eating means no masks. This is the biggest risk I can remember ever taking, and it was my idea. Some of Ted's attitude must be rubbing off on me.

I am having trouble remembering the last time I invited anyone to come for a meal. Now, I'm having doubts as to whether my cooking is still up to scratch. I should stick to something I know really well; a simple roast or a pasta dish. Maybe lasagne - that looks complicated but is really a number of simple processes put together. Team that with a nice salad and it should be fine.

Somewhere I even have a nice tablecloth and candles.

Why am I so nervous? I cook myself meals regularly. I eat regularly. What's the difference if another person is going to be here to eat with me? I'm kidding myself. There is a difference. There's a major difference. It's a date - and I'm really not sure I know how to handle a date. But I didn't know if I could handle the Botanical Gardens, and it was a lovely afternoon. So maybe another date won't be so bad. Maybe I will just relax and enjoy eating with a friend, who might one day be more than a friend.

Is that what's happening here? Is Ted a friend? I guess so. Is he becoming something more than a friend? I think so. What on earth will that mean for the life I've created for myself here? What about my safe little cocoon? Was it ever really that safe anyway? I look at all the new picture frames, the place where the vase used to be. Maybe my safe cocoon was only an illusion anyway.

Raging Rats

Dinnertime discussion is, naturally, Ted's new job.

"H3N5+ has a kind of key on the molecule, that the standard H3N5 doesn't," Ted says, between bites of lasagne. "This is what locks into the central nervous system, and from there takes over the whole body. If we could find a way to remove the key, and turn it back into a regular influenza, or to trick the key into locking into something other than the CNS, a dummy we could make, then we would have a cure.

"We're not there yet, but it was our lab that found this much, because our lab was the first one working on it. Others are catching up, of course, and we're all sharing information."

"How long is that likely to take?" I'm suddenly hopeful that our world can go back to the way it was, before the Zedflu, before masks and suits before deadhead neighbours breaking in during the night.

"I don't know. We've identified the key in the virus. We still haven't identified anything to deactivate it. We're working on rat models, but nothing's making any difference yet."

"Rat models. I thought Zedflu couldn't cross species."

"That's another thing Uncle Martin's done. Dad was working on it before he died, too. The key has been copied and spliced on to a virus that rats are susceptible to."

"So what your lab's actually achieved is to make Zedflu for another species," I know it's the kind of thing scientists have to do, but I am imagining multiple ways this could go wrong. "Can the rat version cross species?"

"Possibly, we're not sure. But don't worry, it's very well contained in our lab, and other labs we've shared it with to work on finding a cure."

"Oh, well I hope all those labs all have great containment systems. And your lab, isn't that where your father contracted Zedflu?"

"Yes, but I haven't seen any problems with the containment systems, or any of the safety systems. I still haven't found a way he could possibly have been exposed."

"So, you took the risk, quit a job you loved, and you haven't found an answer to your question anyway?"

"That about sums it up. But maybe I can help cure the worst disease humanity's ever faced. That would provide some pretty good job satisfaction."

"I guess it would. I just worry about how dangerous the job you're doing is."

"With proper safety protocols, I'm not in any more danger than anyone. And watching the diseased rats has made me very aware of how urgent it is to find the cure."

"Watching diseased rats. Now that's a topic of dinner conversation, I never expected."

"Maybe not great dinner conversation, but a very clear warning of what Zedflu can actually do. The deadhead rats are just insane. They have no concern for their own safety, and all they want to do is kill other rats - tear them apart with their teeth and paws."

"That's just gross."

"And they don't feel any pain, so they can lose limbs and keep on attacking."

"That's horrible."

"I'm very glad you had the sense to lock yourself in your bedroom when your neighbour visited that night. After watching what rats are capable of..."

"Well, I'm kind of glad I locked myself safely in my bedroom that night, too. But I would still rather not talk about it while eating."

"I've read your books, they're worse than this."

"I don't write while eating, either."

Ted laughs. "Fair enough, new topic of conversation. The fortress is complete. Do you feel better?"

"Better than what? Better than I did while hiding in my bedroom? I guess I do, but not better than before I knew that a deadhead could break into my house. And definitely not better than I felt before you took a job in the same lab where your father contracted Zedflu."

"So my safety affects how you feel?"

"Well, um."

"I'm flattered."

"Don't be too flattered. I just don't have a lot of friends."

"So, I'm just a friend?"

"Did you want to be something else?"

"Do you want me to be something else?"

Ted leans across the table to kiss me.

Now don't get me wrong. It's not the first time I've been kissed, but it has been a while. I'm feeling very insecure and unsure of myself. But I am sure that I do want this.

We leave the dishes.

Stranger than Fiction

Farnsedale is on the hunt for Cogburn's murderer.

As usual, things have snowballed, and now she is stuck in a caved-in tunnel in a disused gold mine. Of course, her mobile's not getting any reception, but she can use it for a torch until the power runs down. She didn't call for back-up before she went there, which is her usual style, and the reason for most of the drama in my books. Playing it safe would be boring reading.

She obviously can't go back the way she came, but the mine must to have air shafts, she just has to find one, while she still has light to see by.

I need to increase the tension, step up the danger. So, the bad guys, instead of taking the opportunity to run away after they blew up the entrance to the mine, have decided they have to be sure she's dead. They're also looking for an air shaft, searching from above ground.

They're scrambling around above ground, she's walking determinedly below ground, following a mine tunnel. One thing Farnsedale will never do is panic. She's going to calmly and determinedly find her way out. It's a race to see who will find the nearest shaft first.

Farnsedale's reflecting that even dead Cogburn's getting her into more trouble than he's worth. What did she ever see in him anyway? Cogburn is just her latest problematic love interest. Love consistently gets

Farnsedale into trouble, pushes her into situations that cause even more danger than her work alone.

I'm considering having the bad guys get there first. They have to provide a decent challenge, and I did make them competent enough to take Cogburn down in the last book. Besides, I haven't quite pushed Farnsedale to her limit, and the readers can handle a little more tension.

If I get them there first, I have to have Farnsedale prepared to deal with them. There's still too much book to go for her to arrest them yet. (She will arrest them. Farnesdale hasn't killed anyone yet, and I'm keeping that in reserve for some time I really run out of other options for the character.)

The phone rings. Not Farnsedale's, mine. I step back to my reality long enough to see that Ted is calling.

Ted's been asking around the lab to find out how his father was exposed to the infection. He's realised that the only person there who ever worked with his father was Martin Pryce. All of the other staff had been hired since Robert Beare's death.

"I just don't understand," he says. "Why would Martin fire his entire staff? Did he suspect one of them was responsible for Dad's accident?"

"What does Pryce say?" I ask.

"Just that Dad had been working alone one day, and then called him to say he'd been exposed, and that he was going home."

"So, your Dad knew he was exposed and went home to your Mum?"

"No. He'd never have done that. He wouldn't ever have risked Mum, and he didn't do it deliberately. Dad was home with Mum when he found out he had Zedflu. He told me over Evision, before he died."

"So Martin Pryce is lying."

"Yes, but I don't know why."

"And he's still coughing as if he has the virus?"

"Yes."

"None of the other staff were exposed when your father was?"

"Not that anyone's told me. But I don't see why they'd all quit, or why Martin would fire them."

"Ted, I don't know what's going on, and I know you really want to find out about your Dad, but I am very worried. Can't you just go back to your old job, which was already too dangerous?"

"What's Farnsedale doing right now?"

"She's trying to find a way out of an old mine she's been trapped in."

"Is she planning to give up?"

"It's not an option for her."

"Giving up isn't an option for me either."

"Farnsedale is a fictional character."

"But she inspires me."

"You know that's ridiculous."

"Maybe."

"I'd much rather she inspired you to stay safe."

"If I stayed safe, we'd never have met."

He's got me there. Of course, I know, he's not going to give up his search for answers. If he did, he wouldn't be the person I was falling in love with.

"Is there any way to find people who worked there with your father?"

"Martin's got a storeroom - the door to it is in the office behind his desk. That's where he keeps paperwork, records of old projects, the usual stuff that accumulates.

There will be employee records in there. I just need something that seems like a legitimate reason to get in there."

"You haven't been in there?"

"No, if we need old paperwork, Martin gets it himself. Says he has his own filing system and no-one else would ever find anything."

"That's odd. Most people in his position would have a secretary or assistant to do things like filing."

"He's an odd guy."

"So what kind of excuse can you use to get to the files?"

"I'm trying to think of something Farnsedale-esque."

"Farnsedale-esque? That would involve being shot at, blown up and generally mistreated. Why not keep it simple? You could just go in when he's out of his office. He must leave some time. Like when he's coughing on television interviewers."

"There's that. He's off to intimidate the Science Minister about the need for more research funding this afternoon."

"Sounds like an opportunity. Just be careful. If he had anything to do with your father being exposed to the virus, and they'd been friends for ever, then he's not going to have qualms about doing the same to you."

"And, on that happy note, I'd better get back to work. See you tonight?"

"Absolutely."

I'm back to Farnsedale, but part of my mind is still with Ted. How dangerous can it be to check the files? Surely, it's no worse than being in that lab in the first place? I convince myself Ted will be fine.
They're All Dead

Ted has a lot to talk about over dinner. (Yes, he's here for dinner, again. He hasn't moved in, but he hasn't not moved in either. You know how it is. If life was like a Hollywood movie, we'd have met, got together, broken up, gone through endless torture to learn that we belonged together after all. As it is, we're just sort of together, and it seems to have happened naturally, with no great thought or soul searching. He wants to be with me. I want to be with him. We're together. Hollywood has made love far more complicated than it really has to be.)

When Martin Pryce left for his meeting, Ted simply walked into his office, took the key from the desk drawer and went to the file room. So far so good.

He found staff pay and tax records for the time when his father had come out of retirement.

That's where it stopped being straightforward. He started calling the former employees. Some phones were out of service, some rang out, others were answered by people who didn't know the people he was calling. Eventually, one number led him to the daughter of one of the researchers. Her mother had died, after being exposed to the Zedflu virus she was working on.

Ted went to the government death listing site. That's something new since Zedflu. The government now has a site listing both alphabetically and by date of death, everyone who dies. It's too hard to formally notify all of the relatives, and everyone who should know. So the authorities just put it all online. Ted found all of them on the site. Every person working in the lab when his father had been exposed was dead, all except Martin Pryce.

If it were me, I would have given up, walked out and never gone back there.

Ted's different.

He went back to the file room and looked for details of staff who worked there before Zedflu.

Finding the personnel file for a scientist who had retired at the same time as his father, Ted noted the details when he heard the voice behind him.

"What are you doing in here?" Martin Pryce demanded.

"I'm looking for the tax forms I filled out when I started here. The Tax Office called with a query, and I wanted to be sure I filled out the forms correctly," he lied.

"I don't like anyone in my filing system," Pryce had answered, "for just this reason. You're at the wrong filing cabinet. Current files are over here."

He pulled out a draw, took out a file, and handed it to Ted, who thanked him and took the file back to his own office.

Ted continues his story.

"I called Gertrude Katzenstein, and I'm meeting her at the Botanic Gardens tomorrow. She's a bit older than Dad was, but she's still got her marbles from the sound of it. She remembers me."

"Gertrude Katzenstein, that's a mouthful to say. And she's willing to go out to meet you?"

"Professor Gertrude Katzenstein, no less. Dad always called her Trudy. She was head of molecular biology at Queensland Uni, before she went to work with Dad and Martin. And yes, she says she likes to get out occasionally."

"She must have been a good catch for the lab."

"Oh, I'm sure she could have worked anywhere she wanted. Back then, their lab was really prestigious.

They had the best people, the best equipment, the best everything. I don't know where all the money came from, but as a kid I didn't think about things like the funding for my Dad's work."

"So do you think they had an unusual amount of funding? Or there was something odd about it?"

"I don't know. At the time I didn't think about it. Maybe. Some labs get better funding than others, there's Government grants, but there's also private donations. Maybe the work they were doing was getting extra funding from somewhere. Anyway, maybe that's something else Trudy can answer."

I'm quite awed that an elderly lady is willing to go to the Gardens on her own to meet Ted. She likes to get out occasionally. Even old ladies are braver than me, apparently.

Katzenstein's story

We're talking on Evision. Ted is very disturbed by what he's learned from Gertrude Katzenstein.

Martin Pryce had tried to call her out of retirement along with Ted's father. She'd refused.

"She'd been glad to retire," Ted says. "Apparently, Martin had been acting strangely for some time before she finished work there. She said he had a second lab attached to the main one, and he wouldn't tell anyone what he was working on there."

"A second lab? Surely that would be hard to hide?" I wonder if Trudy really does still have here marbles.

"Really, a second lab. You know that storeroom he doesn't like people going into?"

"The one attached to his office? With the files? Where you found out that everyone was dead?"

"That's the one. Trudy says the door to the lab is in there. I didn't see the door when I was in there, but maybe it's behind the filing cabinets. At the time I was only looking for information from the files. Anyway, that room has a door to a stairway that leads to an underground lab - basically a copy of the main lab, but underneath it."

"That's bizarre. A hidden lab? But if Trudy knew about it, it was hardly a secret."

"Everyone who worked there then knew the lab existed, but the staff who work there now don't seem to know about it."

"So, what did he do with the second lab?"

"It was some sort of secret military thing."

"Biological weapons?"

"Supposedly it was about protecting soldiers from biological weapons, but Trudy never knew any specifics. But that's why the lab was so well funded. It was Martin's super-secret sideline that was bringing in the cash. The regular medical research was subsidised by this hush-hush military stuff."

"Does she know if he ever stopped using the second lab?"

"He hadn't when she left. So, she doesn't know what's gone on since, and she doesn't know why it's a big secret now."

"Maybe he's not using it now?"

"Maybe, but why is he so paranoid about people being in that room?"

"And she said he was acting strangely when she retired?"

"Yes. Apparently, everyone respected that he wasn't allowed to share any of his work from the second lab, or talk about it, and that had never been a problem. But then, not long before she retired, he started to get obsessive, accusing people of spying on his work, starting arguments with people over nothing. He was very aggressive about it at times."

"Have I mentioned how much I dislike you working there?"

"I don't really like it either, but I really want to know what happened to my Dad. And I'm starting to wonder what's really going on with the secret lab, or at least what was going on then. Trudy said that was when he started to complain about people going into the room beside the office. It wasn't a storeroom then, he had it set up as a bedroom, so he could sleep there if he worked late. She said he was always there, no matter what time anyone went into the lab he was there before them and was there after them. She thought he might not have gone home at all."

"You are not thinking of going down to this secret lab, are you?"

"Aren't you even slightly curious about what I might find?"

"I'm more than slightly worried about what you might find. What if this secret lab's contaminated with some horrible germ warfare substance? There could be something really horrible down there!"

"I work with Zedflu. I think I know how to handle really horrible substances."

"Can't you just report all this to someone else? The Health Department or someone?"

"The only facts we have are that there's a second lab, and Martin used to do research for the military. Those aren't crimes, and they aren't things to investigate. Anything anyone has beyond those facts is suspicion and speculation. Farnsedale would get some real evidence, wouldn't she?"

"If I killed Farnsedale off in the next book, would that stop you taking risks?"

He laughed. "It probably wouldn't. And I really want to know what's going on. Aren't you curious?"

"Curious, yes. Suicidal, no."

"I'll be careful," he promised.

A Crazy Plan

Today's the day. Ted is going to find his way into the secret lab.

I have a vague connection to Liz Anderson, a producer at the Channel 3 television station. I've contacted her and told her that Dr Martin Pryce's Zedflu work with rat models was really interesting and would make a great news story. Liz was reluctant, because the last time he'd been on her show, he'd coughed all over both presenters, and there had been a panic in the studio. Because I strongly hinted that I knew someone in his lab, and that he was near a breakthrough, she relented and contacted him for an interview.

The interview is today. Martin Pryce is going to be busy all morning. He apparently loves any opportunity to share his predictions of the end of humanity.

I have the tv on, the Pryce interview will be live in a while. I'm watching, to reassure myself he really will be kept busy, while I know Ted is trying to find his way into the lab.

It's been years since I've bitten my fingernails, but right now, they're being bitten down to the quick, and I'm pacing like a caged lion. Ted texts. He's in the lab and found a mountain of paperwork. It's too much to go through this morning. He's going to do what he can and will call me when he is safely out.

I am wondering if I can call Liz and ask her to find a way to delay Martin Pryce from leaving the studio, to give Ted more time, but I can't think of any excuse to give.

Eventually, I make a decision. I text Ted to tell him what I'm doing, and I suit up and get the car keys. I'm going to the studio myself. Not even Farnsedale would do this, or maybe she would. Maybe that's what makes me think of it.

I decide if I'm going to live dangerously anyway, I might as well be totally on the edge. I go to a drive through on the way and get a burger and chips.

By the time I get to the television studio, Ted has texted back telling me not to do it, but also giving me a description of Martin Pryce's car. He's realised I can be as stubborn as he is, obviously.

It's going to be a while, but I can wait. I'm parked across the road from where Pryce will exit the carpark. It's a simple delaying tactic, but it should be an effective one.

I would read a book or something, but I can't take my eyes off the carpark exit. So I eat my junk food, trying to savour the taste, but I think the recipe's changed because all I can really taste is salt and fat. I can feel fat coating the inside of my mouth. This is gross. How did I ever consider this stuff to be food?

He should be on air about now. I wait, drumming my greasy-gloved fingers on the steering wheel, and wondering why I didn't think to get a drink to wash this taste out of my mouth. I'm impatient, but at the same time, I want him delayed in the station as long as possible, so the later he comes out of the carpark the better. This whole thing is about playing for more time.

I wonder what Ted has found. I wonder how the Pryce interview is going. I know there's been no real breakthrough, but I'm sure the journalists will try their best to get something worthwhile from him. Everyone's desperate for some hope of a cure or preventative. There'll be lots of kudos for anyone who helps break the story that the Zedflu horror is over. That story won't be coming today, however.

Cars come and go from the carpark. My stomach is churning, and my nerves are on edge. I've never done anything like this before. Can I really go through with it? I think of Ted, and the risk he might get caught investigating what Martin Pryce is trying so hard to keep secret. Of course, I can do it. I don't really have any other choice.

At last I see his car approaching the exit. I turn on my ignition. As Martin Pryce's dark blue Falcon turns on to the street, I floor my accelerator.

The crash is sickening. I feel like I've been kicked in the chest by a horse, as I'm thrown into the seatbelt. Suddenly everything is white, and I feel like I'm being

smothered as an airbag deploys into my face. I'm
slightly disoriented for a moment, then I check myself.
Apart from what is going to be a massive bruise across
my chest, and a very sore neck, I'm unhurt. I unbuckle
the seatbelt and step out of the car, to have a proper look
at what I've done.

The nose of my car has crushed in the passenger's side of
his car. It looks like both vehicles are fused together.
Before Zedflu, a crowd would have gathered by now.
As it is, a couple of people in suits have appeared on the
footpath to watch the drama.

"I'm so sorry," I say in a tone I hope indicates I really am
very very sorry. "My foot just slipped. Oh this is all my
fault! Are you hurt? Should I call an ambulance?
Someone to check on you?"

"No need for an ambulance," he said. "But we will need
tow trucks, and the police. And I will definitely want
your insurance details."

I dutifully call the police and take as long as I can over
the swapping of names, addresses and insurance details.

The police arrive, our stories are told. I admit
responsibility and say my foot slipped on the accelerator.
I blame the disposable covers on my shoes which have
no real grip on the sole. I couldn't even steer properly to
avoid the accident because my gloves were greasy from
eating greasy chips. I'm sure they've heard similar stories
before, because they don't really question it.

Tow trucks arrive and take both vehicles away. I apologise once more to Martin Pryce as he catches a taxi.

All in all, I've bought Ted an extra two hours.

By coincidence one of the police officers had been at my house the other night. He is very sympathetic about my run of bad luck and offers me a ride home. From the back of the police car, I send Ted a text to warn him Pryce was on the way back.

I take the opportunity to ask the police officer what happened to my neighbour.

"Taser to the head," he says. "It blows their diseased little brains. Then we just stick them in a body bag and send them to the crem."

I idly wonder if I should try to get hold of a taser. I decide against this for two reasons. I don't know how to get hold of illegal weapons, and I am not ever going to be close enough to a deadhead to use one.

Safely home again, I grieve the loss of my car which will undoubtedly be written off and wait anxiously to hear from Ted.

The Secrets of the Second Lab

We are in my writing room, with endless photographs of documents on my computer. The chalkboard-painted wall behind us has been cleaned of all my writing notes, so we can put notes there if we need to.

Ted didn't waste any time in the secret lab. He found a file cabinet in there, and photographed every page he could, until I warned him that Martin Pryce was on the way back. He has copies of numerous files and of Martin Pryce's personal diary. He tells me Pryce has been clearly living in the second lab. There's a bed down there, clothes and toiletries.

Mentally, I add up all of the crimes we've committed today. From my dangerous driving to Ted's trespass and theft of information. Given that some of what we're looking at probably relates to secret military research, we're probably taking part in treason or espionage or something of that ilk as well.

I'm not really sure what we're looking for, except that maybe the answer as to how or why Ted's father was infected may be in here.

After an hour of scanning endless medical and scientific jargon, with no sign of H3N5+ or anything else I recognise, I announce I'm going to cook dinner. Ted agrees that food would be an excellent idea, and I leave him working.

On the way to the kitchen, I hear the buzzer from the front gate. I check the monitor, there's someone in a suit holding a package.

"Hello," I say into the microphone.

"Package for A. Tynehurst and E. Beare," the man at the gate says.

I'm surprised. I can't think of anyone who would know Ted was here. Maybe he's told someone where to find him. I'll have to ask.

"In the lockbox, thanks," I say. "The number's 7251."

"OK. Have a nice day," the delivery man says as he waves to the camera.

"You too," I respond.

I continue to the kitchen where I cook a couple of steaks and prepare a salad.

I call Ted for dinner. He comes in tilting his head to one side and then the other to stretch his neck.

"Find anything of any use?" I ask, as he sits at the table.

"It looks like his military research was on antivirals, particularly anti-influenza drugs."

"Those could be useful about now," I say. "But why were the military wanting research on it years ago?"

"The flu can be a real problem. It's not just Zedflu. In the first world war, Spanish Flu killed more people than the war did. That could be a problem for any army."

"Could any of his work from then help now?"

"I don't know. It's worth looking at, but if so, why would he sit on it? We're desperate for anything to help now. I'm sure if he asked permission, the military would approve using their stuff to combat Zedflu."

"One would hope so. Surely an army full of homicidal zombies wouldn't be of much use."

I remember the parcel and tell Ted about it. He doesn't know who it would be from, either, but it's been more than 30 minutes, so he goes out to get it from our side of the lockbox, while I clear the dinner table.

It's small, not much larger than a jewellery box. Ted cuts through the tape with a kitchen knife and opens the box.

Suddenly there's a hissing noise, and Ted is on the floor, coughing and choking. "Stay back," he gasps, but his warning is too late. I'm further back, but I have still breathed it in as well, I begin to cough too, though not as badly as Ted. I pull up the tablecloth around the box, wrapping as quickly as I can, and I take it to the hazardous waste chute to dispose of it.

We're both over the initial coughing fit and I ask, "What was that?"

"My guess," Ted says gravely, "is aerosolized Zedflu."

"But the parcel sat for more than half an hour. Zedflu can't live outside the body that long."

"It can if it's not exposed to air."

"Like in your lab."

"Like in my lab."

"Martin Pryce knows what we've done?"

"That would be my guess. Maybe I left something out of place in the secret lab. That, with your accident. He added two and two and got four."

"I suppose we know how your parents were infected now."

"I guess so. Although, I spoke to Dad before he died. He didn't tell me he'd been deliberately infected. Surely he would have said if something like this had happened."

"Maybe he wanted to protect you. He didn't want you doing what we just did, and put yourself in this danger."

"Maybe. We'll never know, because it's too late to ask him now."

"So do we call the Health Department now?"

"No. There's nothing anyone can do for us. But this means Martin really does have something to hide. We need use whatever time we have to find his secret. There's something in those files. There's got to be. Otherwise there'd be no point in infecting us."

I have been so careful for so long, and none of it has mattered at all.

"Print those pages off. We can manage them better on paper," I say. "If I'm going to die over this, I damn well want to know why."

While the papers are printing, I get an Evision call from Liz. She thanks me for the tip-off about Martin Pryce's research. Not that there was much exciting, and new to talk about, but the idea that they'd made Zedflu for another species was just as horrifying to her, and presumably to viewers, as it had been to me. She says Martin Pryce was interested to know who had suggested the interview and was surprised that I had known someone working in his lab. I tell her I may have a much bigger story for her soon but refuse to go tell her any more now. "Just look out for my email," I say, as I end the call.

Martin Pryce knows I was responsible for him being at the Channel 3 studio, and that I am close to someone at his lab. He knows I caused the car accident. He's already caught Ted in the file room. He has far more information than we realised. If there had been any doubt about who sent the parcel, it's gone now. Pryce really does have something to hide and I only hope we have his secret in the information we're printing.

A Mountain of Paper

Ted has the records of experiments and other scientific notes. I have Martin Pryce's journal.

We've put a rough timeline on the blackboard, filling in details as we go.

My headache is still mild, but I can tell Ted's fighting severe pain. He's refusing any painkillers because he wants to be able to focus on what he's reading.

It's been two days since we were infected and if either of us were in any doubt, we're both absolutely certain now that we have Zedflu. We're both sniffing and coughing our way through tissues. I'm feeling alternately hot and cold, and I can see Ted shivering in a cold sweat. Neither of us is willing to give up our search for answers.

From what we can tell so far, Pryce finished his work on antivirals for the military about the same time as Ted's father retired. His work didn't stop there, however. He kept experimenting with various forms of influenza on his own, while his other lab did further, legitimate, research.

Pryce's private work had taken a definitely sinister turn. He wasn't looking at cures.

As I read his journal, rants about how the world would be better off without humans happen more and more frequently. He wrote at great length about how nature was reclaiming the environment from humans in places like Fukushima, where humans had been forced to leave.

I feel sick, and it's not just the flu, as I read his own words about how he considers humankind to be "vermin infesting the planet." Well, Ted did say Pryce had been looking forward to the end of the world for a long time.

Nearing the end of the journal, I find an entry about "the perfect welcome home gift for Mary M."

I look at the date. It's about a week before Mary Elizabeth Marsdensen became famous for all the wrong reasons.

"Ted..." I start to say."

"He created Zedflu," Ted responds. "It's all in here."

"Created it and released it. He infected Mary Marsdensen. He met her at the airport when she was returning from overseas and gave her the virus somehow. But I don't see how he wasn't infected."

"I do. He didn't just create the virus. He created a prophylactic, a kind of vaccine. He's made himself immune. It's not a great vaccine, because it's got side effects, but it does leave him immune."

"So all humans are vermin, except him?"

"Apparently." Ted has a fit of coughing. I recognise the rattling sound he makes. "And not only that. Our rat models, he made those first - the rat form of Zedflu predates the real thing. All the stuff I've been studying with the team, he already knew before now, because he created it. He's controlled everything right from the start. He's sabotaged the whole research program by being first to start studying it and feeding information to other labs that started their work later. He's set the whole research agenda, when he already had the answers."

We know everything we're going to find from the papers. I insist Ted has some painkillers and rests. His joint pain is so bad, I have to help him walk to the bedroom. I bring him tea and painkillers and sponge down his forehead. He is burning up with fever. How did I not notice how sick he had become?

I know he can't have long left. Feeling utterly useless, I sit on the bed beside him and hold his hand. Eventually he drifts off to sleep.

I have the cough now as well, and my head is killing me.

I may have slightly longer than Ted. He was, after all, hit directly in the face with a massive dose of the virus. I don't have much longer, though. I have to decide what I am going to do with this information we're giving our lives for.

As always, I need to make a list.

I sit on the bed, thinking and writing, but we have worked on this for days, and I am exhausted as well as sick. I fall asleep.

Up in Flames

Well, Hollywood didn't just lie about zombies, did it? It lied about love and life and happily ever after as well.

When I wake up, Ted is no longer breathing. He's cold to touch. Looking at the clock, I realise I've slept for fifteen hours straight. It's night.

Ted looks like he's sleeping, like he'll wake up in the morning. Actually, unless I do something he will. And that won't be good.

I could just call the Health Management Team, but my headache is becoming unbearable now, and I have too much to do before I can be taken as well.

There is a little time, at least until tomorrow morning, to do everything that has to be done. I look at my list. It's actually extremely short. First is to tell the world the information Ted gave his life for, the reason his father died. Second is to make sure we don't become deadheads.

Being moderately famous, I know that once I put something on social media, at least a few people will read it, and with what I've got to post now, that few will be enough to make it go viral.

I write:

A dear friend of mine has just given his life to find out the truth about Zedflu. Dr Edward (Ted) Beare went to work in the same lab where his father, Dr Robert Beare (of the Pryce-Beare study) had contracted the H3N5+ virus.

The truth is this:

Dr Martin Pryce is responsible for the development of the H3N5+ virus. He created it, using the far less dangerous H3N5 virus. He also made a non-lethal version which he inoculated himself with, so as to not be able to contract the version which has caused so much trauma to so many people. The non-lethal version has left him with a persistent cough, but no other apparent symptoms, and has the potential to be a base for a useable vaccine to prevent further people catching the disease.

Dr Pryce released the fatal version of the virus at the International Terminal of the Brisbane airport, ensuring spread throughout the world, before it was detected.

He knew exactly what his creation would do, and expected it to cause the extinction of the human race.

By taking a lead in researching the virus, he has been able to undermine efforts to find a cure.

The world needs to know this.

Authorities need to know, so as to ensure Martin Pryce faces justice.

Scientists need to know, because the information hidden in his lab can help prevent further deaths, and all that comes with those deaths. This information is in a second, secret lab, accessed through his office in the lab that everyone knows about.

Ordinary people need to know, and knowing what one person has done, have hope that other people will be able to undo it.

I share it on every form of social media I use.

Then I email that same information and all of Ted's photos of files from the secret lab to Liz at the television station. I tell her about the secret lab, and how it can be found. I give her every detail I can think of that will help her break the story.

I could send the information to someone at Queensland Health instead of to my media contact, but if the foremost researcher in the field is actually trying to kill off the human race, I don't know whether or not I can trust whoever would receive my email. Liz, I know, will tell the story, and will make sure everyone in authority answers to the public for what happens from here.

I guess that's my epitaph. I could wait and watch the reaction. I have time, but I may as well get on with what has to be done.

I collect a can of lawnmower fuel from the shed in the back yard.

Next, I make sure all the doors and windows are closed and the air conditioner is off. I tuck towels under the doors, to make sure there are no drafts, no air moving anywhere in the house.

I turn on all of the gas jets on the stove, without lighting them.

I take all the candles I can find to the bedroom, melt the bottoms to stick them to the bedside table, the dressing table, the top of the chest of drawers, and I light them all. We may not have much of a funeral, but we're going out with a bang.

As the gas starts to build up, while I can still breathe I go through the medicine drawer and take every pain killer or sleeping pill I can find.

Then just to be sure that when the gas reaches its ignition point, the explosion and fire will do its job properly, I pour the mower fuel over the bed.

I open the bedroom window just a tiny bit. I want the house full of gas, but ignition will require a supply of oxygen from somewhere as well.

I think for a moment about electrocuting our brains for extra insurance, like the police officers with tasers, but my headache is unbearable, the drugs are starting to take effect, and my brain is beyond processing how to do that. Maybe I should have tried to get hold of a taser after all. It's too late now.

I look at Ted and sigh. I had not expected to find love, but having done so, I feel cheated of time to build a life together. It's too late. It's far too late for anything now.

Drowsy, and a little nauseous, I climb into the bed. I kiss Ted one last time and drift off to sleep.

More by this Author

You can find more by Iris Carden at
www.lulu.com/spotlight/IrisCarden

www.ingramcontent.com/pod-product-compliance
Lightning Source LLC
Chambersburg PA
CBHW070606180626
46817CB00005B/2015